LIAR, LIAR, PANTS ON FIRE!

Susie Bonner is a town girl right down to the tips of her toes but mum has decided to move to the country and life in a small place is not to Susie's taste. To keep up her spirits Susie writes regularly to her best friend Marsha with an account of her new life, but Susie has a vivid imagination and can't help adding drama to her letters. So when Marsha comes to stay and sees village life as it really is, well things get a bit difficult.

An amusing, perceptive tale from the master of comedy Jeremy Strong.

OTHER BOOKS BY JEREMY STRONG

JEREMY STRONG

Liar, Liar, Pants on Fire!

BARN OWL BOOKS

Originally published in 1988 by A & C Black
This edition published in 2004 by Barn Owl Books
157 Fortis Green Road, London N10 3 LX
Barn Owl books are distributed by Frances Lincoln
4 Torriano Mews, Torriano Avenue, London NW5 2RZ

Copyright © Jeremy Strong 1988 and 2004

ISBN 1-903015-37-5

Designed and typeset by Douglas Martin
Printed and bound in China for Imago

Chapter One

A new place — a few lies

From her bedroom window Susie could see a hill. It was a long, high hill with fields and hedges stretching almost half-way up and then there were trees and more trees until the sky took over. Spring was well on its way. There was a hurry of green and rush of birds everywhere.

Susie hated it. She would never understand why her mother had wanted to move here after Dad had left home and gone to live with somebody else. In the last house she had been used to the continuous hum of traffic, voices, people and endless movement. It had made her move, caught by the currents of city life, and drawn her out of the upstairs flat and down into the road. She would wander the city backstreets, arm in arm with her friend Marsha, calling out to people they knew. They would run and laugh and dodge the traffic and sit on doorsteps for hours, talking and giggling.

Susie looked at the long, quiet hillside, dotted with a few cows and wondered bitterly if anything, ANYTHING, had ever happened to that hill. Had there ever been a battle, with soldiers being cut down in pools of blood. Had a plane carrying four hundred passengers ever crashed into it, exploding in a ball of flame? It was hardly likely.

A flock of wood pigeons launched themselves from the wood, their wings clattering like castanets. They wheeled away over the horzon. Susie groaned to herself. Wow! That *was* exciting. She left the window and went downstairs. Her mother was soaking some beans. 'I've just seen some pigeons!' Susie announced, with as much enthusiasm as possible.

Mrs Bonner hardly glanced at her daughter. 'You'll get used to it. This place is different, that's all. Why don't you go outside? Maybe you'll find something good to do. Of course you'll be bored if you stay upstairs staring out of the window.'

'But there isn't anything to do,' muttered

Susie.

'I've found plenty,' replied Mrs Bonner. Susie glanced at the kidney beans her mother was soaking, red and shining in a pan of cold water. They looked like little baby fish, all fat and ready to wriggle.

'Are they for lunch?' Susie asked

'There's salad and soup as well.'

'I wish I could have beefburgers, or sausages . . .'

'It's salad and soup today. I've just told you.' Mrs Bonner banged the pan on the cooker and some water spilt over the edge.

'When are you going to stop your diet?' Susie asked. Her mother always seemed to be on a diet. Susie would not have minded except that she always had to eat what her mother ate.

'Did you say you were going out?' suggested Mrs Bonner coldly.

'Going.'

Mrs Bonner called Susie back from the door, 'Try and make some new friends. We've been in this house for three weeks and you still haven't got to know anybody. Still, you'll soon make new friends when school starts after the holiday."

That was the last thing Susie wanted to hear, and she hurried outside. She was dreading the start of school – all the new teachers, new children, new buildings. It was impossible to imagine what it would be like. Susie had never moved house before, or changed school. It was such a titchy school too – like in Toytown – and certainly very different from the big one she had come from.

Susie walked slowly down to the river. It was only a small river, almost narrow enough to jump over, but not quite. There was a little waterfall where the water splashed and sparkled over a wooden floodgate. Susie leaned on the railings and watched. Some children were playing near it, scrabbling about in the water by their feet. Every now and then one would plunge his hands into the water and grunt.

'What are you doing?' asked Susie.

'Don't be nosy,' answered a tall boy with dark hair and a long, thin face. He stood up and stared at Susie. She stared back at him.

'So what are you staring at then?' demanded the boy.

'What are you staring at?' countered Susie.

'You.'

'Makes two of us then, doesn't it?' replied Susie cheerfully. This was the sort of game she was well used to.

'Get lost!' shouted the boy.

'Free country – I can do what I like.'

'I said get lost!' He began to wade towards her, but the other children had stopped to watch this battle of wits and one of them put out a hand to touch the tall boy.

'Leave her alone John. She hasn't done anything.'

'She's staring at me,' John scowled.

'Cat can look at a king,' murmured Susie, already losing interest in her quarrel. She wanted to know what they were up to, fiddling about in the water. 'What are you doing?' she repeated.

'Fishing,' said one of the girls. 'Looking for crayfish.'

'What are crayfish?'

The tall boy grinned and laughed. 'She doesn't know what crayfish are. What a wally!'

Some of the others laughed too and they stood up straight and looked at Susie as if she had just arrived from another planet. Susie found this hard to take and she turned back up the path. She could hear the children in the river still laughing. This village was the most horrible place she had ever come across. Why her mother wanted to live here she just did not know.

And there was the hill again. You could see it from the street. Hills, sky, river, birds and children who laughed at her. That was what this village was all about. She hated it.

'Did you find anything?' asked Mrs Bonner when Susie got back. 'Did you see anyone to play with?'

'No.' Susie flung herself down in a chair.

'Here, put these on the table. Lunch is ready.'

Susie groaned and got up again. 'What are crayfish?' she asked.

'Crayfish? A kind of lobster, I think. Why do you ask?'

'Some children at the river were trying to catch them.'

'Are there crayfish in the river? What a fantastic place this is,' said Mrs Bonner, grinning at her daughter like an eight year old. She sat down at the table. 'I really do like this place.'

After that there was silence until Mrs Bonner asked Susie what she was going to do with the afternoon.

'Don't know,' Susie stared down at her beans and salad. Life was rapidly becoming dull and horrible. 'There isn't anything to do.'

'Why not write a letter to Marsha? Maybe her parents will let her come and stay sometime.'

Susie dropped her fork. 'Stay? Here? When?'

'Don't get so excited. Sometime in the future when we are more settled – during the next holidays maybe – if her mum and dad will let her.'

'Of course they will.'

'In that case you'd better write and ask, hadn't you?' Mrs Bonner was secretly pleased to see Susie excited for once. She was beginning over the place.

After lunch Susie went upstairs and found a piece of paper and a biro. She stared out of the window at the the hill for a while. She couldn't tell Marsha what a dump her new home was, or she would never come. Besides, Susie wasn't going to admit to her best friend that she had moved to the most boring place in the universe.

Dear Marsha,

I have settled into my new home well. I hope you are well and I won't forget you. You can come to stay the night mum says so ask your mum if you can. I have been exploring the village and it is really good. There is a river with rapids and a waterfall that is really big. You can stand behind the waterfall and hide behind the water. It's really good and I have been swimming in the river and caught some crayfish. They are like giant lobsters and dangerous but you have to know how to catch them and I do.

Lots of love
Susie.

Chapter Two

A new school – another lie

Mrs Bonner took Susie to school on her first day. Susie wished she hadn't. In the city it wasn't so bad – Mum didn't stick out in the city because there were so many different-looking people around. But in a little village like this Mrs Bonner was bound to stand out.

For a start she was obviously younger than most of the other mothers who turned up with their children on that first morning of the new term. They had smart coats and smart hair and smart smiles to match. And there was Mrs Bonner with her black leather mini-skirt, red tights, high heels and sunglasses. It was April, and the sun was about as bright as a birthday candle.

People stared. Susie wanted to be a thousand miles away. She knew that people were whispering behind her back, but Mrs Bonner took no notice and went round to the office with Susie.

'I'll come and pick you up,' she said cheerfully, and Susie realised that her mother *knew* everyone was looking at her, and she enjoyed it.

'No – it's all right. I'll walk back.'

Mrs Bonner bent down and kissed Susie on the cheek. 'Don't be silly. Not on your first day – I'll be by the gate. 'Bye for now. Be good!' She turned and walked away with a little grin on her face. Her eyes, hidden by the dark glasses, darted about, examining the other parents. Straight past the whole lot she walked, smiling to herself as her ear caught bits of whispers like dirty cobwebs: 'skirt – look at her – sunglasses – what a sight –'

In school Susie found herself at a table with three others: Mark, Alan and Kiki. They soon discovered where she lived and Alan said something about council houses and added that he lived in the big house at the end of the private road near the church and did Susie know where he meant?

'I only know the river bit,' said Susie, shaking her head.

'Was that your mum who brought you to school?' asked Kiki.

'What does your dad do?' asked Mark.

'I haven't got a dad.' The others looked at her so oddly Susie didn't dare tell them the truth. She plunged on quickly. 'He was killed.'

'Killed? What do you mean?'

'Got run over by a bus.'

There was silence. Kiki shuffled her feet. 'That's awful,' she murmured at last. Susie fiddled with her pencil and went a bit red. She was staggered by her own lie and wished they could talk about something else.

'What does your dad do?' she asked desperately of Mark.

'He's a sort of manager and he has to go away quite a lot on business. He's quite important Mum says because he's got a car with electric windows from the firm as a sort of present she says.'

Susie wished she hadn't asked.

Alan butted in. 'But he's only a manager, isn't

he? He works for the firm.'

'It's a very big firm,' said Mark.

'My dad works for himself,' said Alan proudly. 'He takes people's money and uses it to make lots more money for them and then he gets some of it. He's brilliant and he's got a Porsche and a vintage Rolls.'

Susie wasn't so sure what a vintage Rolls was. She had some vague picture of a mouldy cheese roll mounted on a velvet cushion in a glass case. Somehow the idea didn't seem right.

'His dad's gots pots of money,' explained Kiki. 'They went skiing and they went to America at Christmas for a holiday.'

'I got jet-lag,' declared Alan with a grin.

'What's jet-lag?' asked Susie.

'The time changes when you go to America and . . .'

'Why?'

Alan stared at Susie. Nobody had ever asked him before. 'I don't know. It just does. The time changes and it's earlier and that means you stay up longer and get more tired. Then when you come back it changes again and it's even worse.

It makes you feel really tired. It's just something you have to put up with when you go to the States.' Alan made it sound as if he were showing off a terrible operation scar, but Susie still didn't understand and anyway, she was quite well aware that Alan was simply boasting.

Shortly before lunch Susie's teacher, Mrs Templeton, quietly took her to one side. 'I was so sorry to hear about your father,' she said sympathetically. 'Did it happen long ago? Would you like to talk about it?'

'No!' It was the last thing Susie wanted to discuss. She swallowed hard and shook her head. Mrs Templeton gave a little smile.

'If ever you do, you can come to me,' she said kindly. 'Remember that, won't you?'

Susie nodded desperately, wishing she could run to the end of the earth. Her teacher nodded too and moved away. Susie heaved a huge sigh of relief. Her heart was thundering beneath her ribs. It took half the lunch-hour before she calmed down.

The rest of the day passed reasonably well, but Susie was glad when school was finished.

Mrs Bonner was waiting by the school gate. She smiled and waved when she saw Susie. 'Have a good day? Make any friends?'

Susie shrugged and tried to hurry her mother away from the school. Teachers were coming out and Mrs Templeton was looking her way, obviously trying to make up her mind about coming over.

'Is that your teacher?' asked Mrs Bonner.

'Yes,' hissed Susie.

Mrs Bonner nodded and smiled and Mrs Templeton came across.

'You must be Susie's mother,' she began.

'Mrs Bonner.'

'Yes, I'm sorry . . .' Mrs Templeton dropped her voice low as if Susie shouldn't hear. 'I'm sorry about your husband . . .'

'I'm glad he's gone,' said Mrs Bonner.

Mrs Templeton was so taken aback, she was momentarily speechless. She looked curiously at Mrs Bonner and Susie, who was still staring hard at the ground and wishing she could go home. 'Well, um, I hope Susie has had a good day at school.'

'She'll soon settle down,' declared Mrs Bonner. Car doors were slamming as parents drove their children away. 'Come on, Susie.'

They started to walk away from the school. the noise of parents and children and cars got left behind as they headed for home. Mrs Bonner kept up a non-stop chatter all the way back.

'Look at that house Susie, three garages, let alone a double one. These are three-car families, not just two. Do you know what we are? We're a two-shoe family – one for each foot. Still, who cares? Nice round here isn't it? Beats that filthy town. Nice and quiet. I saw some funny birds this morning, big and black and white they were, with a long tail.'

'They were magpies,' murmered Susie.

'Magpies! Never seen one of them before. How do you know they were?'

'I learnt it at school – my last school. We had the rhyme to learn. *One for sorrow, two for joy, three for a girl, four for a boy, five for* . . . I've forgotten the rest.'

'Just my luck! I saw four this morning. Four

for a boy Here, I don't want to be pregnant, let alone have a boy. Heaven forbid!'

'You're supposed to salute to break the spell,' added Susie helpfully, and she had to laugh as her mother stood in the middle of the pavement saluting. First there was a soldier's salute, then a Nazi salute and a cub salute and then salutes with two hands. It looked as if she was trying to fly.

'Come on,' said Susie, as she saw several people stopping to stare. Her mother was obviously in one of her excited moods.

'Do you think that's enough to break the spell?' asked Mrs Bonner seriously. 'I'm really worried. Four for a boy – what a disaster! It's a good thing you knew the magic charm.'

They finally got indoors without anything else extraordinary happening. Mrs Bonner got some tea – more beans and salad. Susie picked at it half-heartedly.

'It's good for you,' said Mrs Bonner. She finished her plate and sat back, looking across at the tropical fish tank that stood on the sideboard. It was one of the few things Mr Bonner had left behind when he'd walked out. There was only one fish inside, a huge multi-coloured flat-sided fish, an Oscar. It floated almost motionless in the tank, slowly flapping tail and gills. Mrs Bonner went to the tank and bent down. She put her nose by the glass and pulled a face at the fish as it eyed her with big yellow emotionless eyes. 'Typical male chauvinist fish,' muttered Mrs Bonner. 'Just sits there waiting to be fed. Why don't you do the ironing for once?' she shouted at the tank.

Susie slipped her salad and beans into the bin while her mother argued with Oscar.

Chapter Three

One or two discoveries

Dear Susie,

It's really boring here. I wish I could come and stay. It sounds great in your new village. I've never seen a waterfall. Have you caught any giant lobsters yet? My Mum says I might be able to come and stay in the holidays. My brother is being a real pain and we went swimming to the new aqua zoom and he nearly drowned and it serves him right.

Love
Marsha.

P.S. Write again I like getting letters it was my first one.

Mrs Bonner laughed when she saw Marsha's letter. She was puzzled by the waterfall and lobster part and asked Susie to explain. Susie coloured and said it was probably some kind of joke.

'I don't understand Marsha's jokes really,' she added, cheering up as the lie grew stronger in her mind. 'Sometimes she laughs at nothing.'

'I like her,' said Mrs Bonner. 'I hope she can come and stay. She'll like it here in the country. I'll tell you what,' she added, still looking at Marsha's letter, 'I remembered something about crayfish. When we were kids we used to catch them.'

'Like those kids in the river?'

'No – we had jars and string and bacon.' Susie screwed up her face in disbelief. 'It's true.' said Mrs Bonner. 'You tie the string to the jar and put the bacon inside and dangle the whole thing in the river. The crayfish just crawl in and whoosh! You've got one.'

'I'm going to try it,' shouted Susie, racing to the kitchen.

'Sorry, no bacon. You'll have to wait.' Mrs Bonner handed back Marsha's letter and Susie went upstairs, reading it once more. The letter made her uneasy and for the first time in her life Susie felt a twinge of fear about Marsha. It was all that rot about the waterfall and lobsters that did it. Susie felt even more lonely and cut-off than ever. She stared out of the bedroom window.

Slowly her thoughts were taken over by the hill. There it was, same as ever, long and high, unmoving, dotted with cows. All at once Susie decided that she would climb it, right to the top. There was nothing better to do and she *had* to do *something*.

There was a path that started between the houses and then crossed fields, climbing all the time. Susie was soon hot and panting. She sat on a fallen tree, surrounded by cows and looked back at the village below. It was very pretty. A cow snorted nearby and there was a strong, unmistakable animal smell.

'Urgh,' snorted Susie, as she climbed higher up the hill, treading carefully between cow-pats and setting swarms of flies buzzing furiously around them.

At length the path entered the woods. Susie hesitated, then went on, going deeper and deeper into the shadowy darkness beneath the trees. Birds chattered the alarm to each other and branches quivered dramatically as unseen squirrels fled further into the depths of the wood.

Susie couldn't see the village now, only the trees. Here and there massive trees plunged into the sky, their tops exploding with leaves that danced in the sun. Susie was surprised to realise she found it all rather exciting and she walked round the thick trunks, watching the patterns of the branches twist and turn and change above her head.

Suddenly she caught sight of a rope hanging from a tree. Somebody had managed to get it over a branch miles above Susie's head. Now it hung still, almost touching the ground. Susie tugged it, testing the strength. It held firm.

She grasped the rope and swung back, then launched herself forward. In a moment she was swooping through the air, the rope twisting as she went so that the whole wood revolved around her like some magic picture show. Her hair streamed out as the air whistled past her and she laughed out loud, it felt so good.

Then she noticed an old fallen tree and she climbed as high as she could, clutching the rope. She launched out and went zooming down, down, down and WHUMP!! Susie thudded into the ground and almost winded herself. She lay dazed and bruised, looking up at the sky.

'You wally.'

In an instant Susie was on her feet. There was the tall boy with the dark hair and thin face she'd seen in the river. He snatched the rope from her, climbed up the tree and jumped, swinging clear over Susie's head and she ducked and he laughed. Then he dropped to his feet and looked back at her.

'S'easy,' he said, with a cocky grin.

'I know. I can do it,' said Susie, trying to make herself sound like the World Champion Rope-Swinger.

'No you can't. You crashed. You had your hands too low. You've gotta climb up the rope as you jump or you hit the ground, like you did. Lift your legs and climb the rope. That's how you do it,' sneered John.

'I know!' shouted Susie.

'You're a liar,' grinned John and Susie hated his know-all look. 'I bet you can't climb either.'

'Can.'

'Bet you can't.' John seized the rope and began to scramble up. Hand over hand he went, grasping the rope with his feet and pulling himself higher and higher until he reached the branch that Susie thought was a mile high. John looked down and grinned.

'Bet you can't,' he repeated. He sat on the branch and tried to look carefree. 'Anyone could climb it,' he went on. 'S'easy.'

'I know,' retorted Susie, looking up at John with a growing smile. She had nothing to worry about with him right up there out of harm's way. 'That sort of thing is easy for monkeys. I'll bring you a banana next time. See you!' And she turned and fled down the hill, out into the fields and didn't stop until she got to the bottom. She looked back up the path but there was no sign of John. She laughed to herself and ran home.

'You look cheerful,' said Mrs Bonner. 'Have a good time?'

'I found a tree with a rope hanging from it and you can swing. It's like flying, only you don't get jet-lag. I climbed up it too, right to the top. You can sit on the branch. It's great!'

Susie pottered round the room chattering about the tree while Mrs Bonner tried to read her book. 'You're a right monkey,' she said at last and Susie fell silent and went up to her room. She looked at the silent hill and wondered if John was still up the tree. Maybe he could only climb up and not down?

'Stupid wally,' she murmered to herself.

Chapter Four

Fish can't wash up

'How long ago did your dad get killed?' asked Kiki one day at school.

'My dad? Oh I don't know. Just a few months, I suppose.'

'My mum feels really sorry for you. She says it must be awful not having a father and him dying like that. I bet you cried a lot.'

They were walking round the playground. Kiki draped an arm across Susie's shoulder to comfort her. Susie squirmed inside.

'Didn't cry much,' she said.

'Was your mum upset?'

'Yeah.'

'Everybody feels sorry for you. Even Mrs Templeton,' said Kiki, who really did feel sorry for Susie, the girl who'd lost her father. It made her glad to know she was doing her bit to comfort the poor girl.

At last Susie managed to get away and she wandered off, her brain humming like an overloaded computer. There were too many problems: Marsha, Kiki, her mother, her father, the village, school – the list seemed endless.

Straight after school Mrs Bonner said she had to go to the village shop, so Susie went along too. There were quite a few people inside, mostly mothers who had come along with their children after school. They wandered about putting packets of this and that into their baskets, but mostly bumping into each other and standing there chatting while nobody else could get at the shelves.

A tall, rather beautiful lady with long dark hair came over to Mrs Bonner. She smiled gently and said, 'You must be Mrs Bonner, Susie's mother. My daughter has told me all about you.' At that moment Kiki appeared with her five-year-old brother Richard in tow. He was clutching a huge packet of sweets.

'Can I . . .' he began.

'No. Put it back. Kiki, why did you let him find those? You know it always causes trouble.'

Kiki dragged Richard away. 'Yes, Kiki told me all about Susie on her first day at school.'

'I'm glad Susie's made a friend,' said Mrs Bonner, smiling.

'She must come to tea soon.' Mrs Thomson's face suddenly went very serious. 'I was so sorry to hear about your husband. What a tragic accident.'

Susie felt her whole life fall like a broken lift down a bottomless shaft. She turned deathly white.

'What accident?' asked Mrs Bonner.

'Tragic,' repeated Mrs Thomson. 'Getting run over like that.'

Susie's mother stared at Kiki's mother for several seconds, then she gave a huge laugh. 'Run over! He didn't get run over. He ran off, that's what he did. He ran off with some cow and good riddance to him. Got some peace and quiet now, I have, and my freedom.'

It was Mrs Thomson's turn to stare – along with everyone else in the shop who had heard. 'Oh, sorry. I must rush,' she muttered, hastily grabbing her children and leaving. Richard wondered why anyone would want to run off with a cow.

'It wasn't a real cow,' snapped Mrs Thomson, and she turned to Kiki.

'You said Susie's father had been killed by a bus!'

'He was. She said he was. That's what Susie said.'

'Are you sure you haven't been making it up?'

'Yes!' Kiki was almost in tears. Mrs Thomson pushed her children into the car and started the engine.

'So Susie was lying. Poor child – what she must be going through.'

Back at the shop Susie was following her mother like a zombie. Mrs Bonner was still laughing to herself, unaware of the other shoppers staring and whispering. It was a nightmare for Susie. At last Mrs Bonner finished and they walked home. She seemed to have no idea that Susie was the creator of the lie. Perhaps she thought somebody had just misheard the real story.

Anyway, Susie didn't feel like hanging about just in case her mother did find out. She grabbed her jacket and set off for the hilltop.

As the houses disappeared and the silent countryside swallowed her up, Susie felt relief. She didn't have to talk or explain anything. She marched up the hillside without looking back and did not slow down until she got near the big tree with the rope. She approached carefully, fearful lest John was there. He wasn't.

Susie stared up at the thick branch over her head. Then she started to climb, hand over hand. Her feet flapped about in the air trying to grab the rope. She felt it between them, then it was gone. Her arms were being dragged from their sockets. She waggled her legs frantically, then gave up and fell to earth. She sat there, staring at the leaf mould, then she stood up and had another go. It was no use.

Susie decided to have a few goes at swinging instead. She did what John had said and grasped the rope higher up. It was quite true. By swinging her legs up high she passed over the ground without dive-bombing it as she had last time. She stayed up on the hilltop for almost an hour. She found a strong bit of wood and tied the rope round it so that it made a little seat. She even managed to stand on it a couple of times, which was very difficult and did a lot to restore her sense of pride.

When she got home tea was already on the table.

'Where have you been?' asked Mrs Bonner and Susie told her.

'All this time? By yourself? Weren't you lonely?

'It was great.'

'Kiki's mother has asked if you'd like to have tea there. Are you friends with Kiki?'

'Sort of. She sits next to me at school.' Susie felt rather uneasy about Kiki, especially now that she'd heard about Dad walking out and leaving them.

Mrs Bonner was already thinking about something else. She was looking at the fish tank, as she often did. 'There's one difference between Oscar and a man,' she said to Susie. 'I know they're both utterly lazy, bone idle and stupid and want to be waited on hand and foot – or should I say fin and tail?'

'What's the difference?' asked Susie.

Mrs Bonner smiled, pleased with herself. 'Oscar doesn't talk. He just lies there in the water. He doesn't argue or answer back. He doesn't shout or throw things. He's a very quiet chauvinist.'

'What is a chauvinist?' asked Susie, who'd heard her mother use the word more times than she cared to remember.

'Your father,' said Mrs Bonner darkly, and she got the dirty plates together and took them to the sink. She turned and grinned at Susie, waving the plates in the air like raffle prizes. 'Surprise, surprise! It's washing-up time again!'

Mrs Bonner went quiet and still, staring down at the dishes. The smile faded from her face. She lifted one dirty plate from the sink and went to the fish tank, while Susie watched the drama unfold, holding her breath as the air in the kitchen seemed to suddenly tighten around her.

Mrs Bonner slipped the dirty plate into the

tank, 'You can't walk out on me, can you, you floating sponge. Time you did the washing-up for a change, Oscar my man,' she hissed. 'Come on. Let's see you work for your supper.'

'Mum, what are you doing?'

Oscar drifted gently over to the plate. A few dirty crumbs released themselves and floated to the surface. The giant fish swallowed one, spat it out, turned his tail on the plate and continued to stare out of the tank at Mrs Bonner. She stood up and took the plate from the tank. She went back to the sink and began the washing-up. Susie was shocked to see how her mother's bright face had collapsed and thought she might even be crying.

Susie quietly left the room and went upstairs to think. Surely Dad hadn't been that terrible. And if Mum really was pleased that he'd gone, why was she so upset about it?

Chapter Five

Liar! Liar!

Dear Marsha,
   When are you coming to stay? I really miss you. It will be really good. I wish I had a brother or sister to play with. There's a big boy in the village and he picks fights and pushes people around. I don't like him but it's brilliant in the woods. There's a rope and you can swing from it for miles and climb up it to a tree-house and sit there and have picnics. It's ace.
      Love from
         Susie.

Susie folded the paper and pushed it into an envelope. A tree house would be really good, she thought. She could just picture herself up there, looking out over the forest, queen of everything in sight. Along comes John and she grabs the rope and pulls it into the tree. John stands below waving his fist and shouting, quite unable to get at her. Susie grinned and stuck the envelope flap. She went downstairs to ask for a stamp.

'You'll have to get one at the Post Office. Can you feed that monster before you go out?', asked her mother.

Susie got the little tub of fish food and sprinkled some on to the surface of the water. Oscar rose slowly and opened his big mouth and the food vanished.

Mrs Bonner watched her daughter. 'Just like your father to leave that thing behind. Couldn't leave anything useful, could he?'

'Will he come back?' Susie asked quietly, watching the fish.

'Not if I have anything to do with it.'

Susie bit her lip. She couldn't understand why her mother didn't want him back. That's what people were supposed to be: mums and dads and children – together.

Mrs Bonner went over to Susie and hugged her. 'It's not that easy,' she said. 'I know what you're thinking, but your father and me – well . . .' Mrs Bonner couldn't think of the words. She caught sight of Oscar floating in his silent luxury. 'It was like being married to that fish,' she said at last and laughed and hoped Susie would understand.

But Susie didn't. She took some money for a stamp and went down to the Post Office. All Susie knew was that Mum didn't want Dad back. She had no idea what her father wanted because she had only heard from him once since he had walked out three months earlier. The postcard had just said he was sorry and that he loved her but it was better this way . . . Susie still had it, rather tear-stained, in her bedroom in a secret place.

'You're a liar,' a voice jerked her from her thoughts. It was Alan.

'Don't know what you're talking about.'

'Liar! Liar! Pants on fire!' chanted Alan. 'You said your dad was dead, only he isn't. Gone off with somebody else, hasn't he? My mum says she's not surprised either seeing as how your mum looks.'

'Shut up!'

'Oh wow! Who do you think you are? The prime minister? You're the liar, not me.'

'Get lost!'

'Liar! Liar! Pants on fire! Wait until I tell everyone at school!'

'Alan, I'm going. Come on.' There was a call from a parked car. Alan grinned meanly at Susie and walked off, hands in pockets.

Susie crept into the Post Office like a common thief, bought her stamp, posted the letter and ran home like the wind.

'You were quick,' said Mrs Bonner, as Susie threw herself panting into a chair. 'I remembered after you went off – I've got some bacon. Bought it yesterday and forgot all about it.'

Susie was already up out of the chair. 'Have we got a jar?'

Her mother went to a cupboard. 'Ta-ra!' she cried, holding out a small glass jar. She got a piece of string and showed Susie how to tie it round the neck of the jar.

'Then you just put a little bit of bacon inside and let the whole thing sink to the bottom of the river.'

'Great. Thanks!' Susie was already out of the door.

'Hang on Susie! I'm coming too.'

There was no one else down at the river and Susie was glad. She took her shoes and socks off and waded in. The cold made her draw breath and Mrs Bonner sat on the side and laughed. Once the mud had settled Susie let the jar fill with water and sink down. She bent over it, watching like an eagle. A stone moved. It moved again. The stone sort of scampered sideways. It wasn't a stone. 'I can see one! I can see one!'

The crayfish pushed its feelers over the edge of the jar. A moment later it had crawled in and Susie was plunging back to the side in triumph. She held the jar up as Mrs Bonner inspected it. 'That's a crayfish all right,' she said with a big grin. 'I said it would work, didn't I?'

'I didn't really believe you,' admitted Susie. 'It sounded daft.'

Mrs Bonner looked at Susie very seriously. 'But crayfish *are* daft! That's why it works so well. At least, this one's daft.'

'He's a real wally,' laughed Susie, tipping the crayfish back into the river. 'Now I'm going to catch some more.'

They stayed by the water for almost an hour, by which time Susie had caught over twenty crayfish. Mrs Bonner was sure some had been caught two or three times. 'They never learn,' she said as they walked back up the road. 'Here, is that our phone ringing? Quick, where's the door key?'

They got in just in time and Mrs Bonner snatched up the phone, and answered, panting. It was Kiki's mother, Mrs Thomson, asking if Susie would like to come for tea after school the next day. Susie gritted her teeth and prayed that her mother would say no. They had had such fun down by the river and now suddenly it was the Post Office scene all over again and all the problems that went with it. Why hadn't she kept her big mouth shut, or at least told the truth?

'Yes, she'd love to. That is kind. Thanks very much. Tomorrow. Bye.' Mrs Bonner looked across at Susie. 'She's invited you to tea. That's great. I'm glad you're making new friends. Perhaps Marsha won't need to come and stay after all.'

'But you said!' Susie burst out. 'You said she could!'

'All right, all right, of course she can. It's just nice that you're making friends here too.' She sat down with a sigh.

Susie stood by the sink and looked at the dirty jar and wet string trailing limply over the side. She wondered how she would ever get herself out of the mess she was in. What was going to happen at school tomorrow? There'd be Kiki and Alan – they both knew about her dad and were bound to tell everyone. Then there was Mrs Templeton, she'd know too. What would she say about it? On top of all that she was going to have to go round to Kiki's after school for tea. Susie knew why. It was Mrs Thomson that her mother had shocked in the village store. Susie reckoned she was heading for big trouble all ways round, and she couldn't see any way out of it.

Susie looked over at her mother, sitting back in her chair with her feet up and a relaxed smile on her face. It was more than she could bear. 'I hate this village!' she yelled. 'I hate this house and I hate school and I hate Kiki and I hate crayfish!' Susie stamped across the room, slammed the door behind her and rushed upstairs to her silent, waiting bedroom.

Chapter Six

A new friend?

Susie left going to school until the last minute because she did not wish to meet anyone in the playground. In fact she was a few minutes late.

'Ah,' said Mrs Templeton, looking up from her desk. 'You are here Susie. Good.'

Susie looked at her teacher carefully, but Mrs Templeton was already sorting out something on her desk. Susie went to her table where Mark and Alan sat grinning at her.

'How's your father?' asked Alan under his breath, and he sniggered.

'Bit squashed is he? Can't be nice being run over by a bus.'

Susie ignored him. She kept her eyes on her book.

'I wonder where her daddy's gone?' hissed Mark. 'Gone away, gone away,' he sang. 'Ow!' His face suddenly screwed up in pain and he

His face suddenly screwed up in pain and he bent low over the desk, thrusting an arm beneath the table to rub his leg.

'She kicked me!'

'No she didn't,' said Kiki. 'I did.'

'You!'

'Yes. Leave her alone.'

Mark started to rise to his feet. 'I'm going to tell Mrs Templeton,' he began.

Kiki smiled back at him. 'Good. Then I'll tell her what you and Alan were saying to Susie.'

Mark stopped, half standing, glaring at Kiki. Mrs Templeton looked across and asked if he wanted anything. 'Can I go to the toilet?' he asked lamely.

Mrs Templeton nodded and Mark left. Kiki grinned at Susie, who was so confused she didn't know what to make of it all. When playtime came, Mrs Templeton called Susie over while the others went outside. 'How old are you now Susie? Ten? Susie nodded. 'Quite a grown-up girl. Do you miss your father?'

Susie looked at the ground. She could not think of an answer, not just like that. There was no way she could put into words all the mud-dle of her mind. She wanted to say yes, yes, I miss my dad. But she didn't – not truly miss him. She didn't feel like those people on TV who wrung their hands and sobbed. She didn't feel sad, but yes, she did miss something. It wasn't her dad and she couldn't say what it was. Susie didn't even know if it was a person or a place or a thing.

'It must have seemed strange moving from a big town to a little village,' went on Mrs Templeton, ignoring Susie's long silence. 'Have you made any friends here?'

'No.'

'Not one?' Susie shook her head. 'I'm sorry to hear about your father. That sort of thing hap-pens sometimes. Was your mother very upset?'

'A bit.'

'Does she think he'll come back?'

'She doesn't want him back'

'Do you want your father back?'

Susie shook her head. 'I don't know.'

Mrs Templeton sat on the edge of her desk and shuffled her feet. 'You didn't need to say your father had been killed in an accident.'

Silence.

'It's just made things worse for you.'

Silence.

'If there's anything I can do to help, let me know, Susie.'

Susie went slowly out to the playground. Kiki was by the outer door, waiting. She wanted to know everything that Mrs Templeton had said, but Susie didn't want to talk. If only she had a friend like Marsha. Marsha understood everything; but Kiki, well, there was no telling what Kiki was up to.

'My mum feels really sorry for you,' began Kiki, draping her arm round Susie's shoulder just as before. 'You're coming to tea tonight, aren't you? We'll have a great time – look out! There's Mark and Alan. Quick, come round this way. They think you're a liar.'

Kiki steered Susie out of sight behind a wall. Susie was thinking she knew the boys thought she was a liar, and they were quite right. She was a liar. In a strange way Susie understood Mark and Alan much better than Kiki. At least she knew what they were thinking and why. She could deal with that, but Kiki didn't behave like a normal person at all.

For the rest of the day Kiki protected Susie from other children. She was proud of her success and felt she was doing a very good thing. Then it was time to go to Kiki's for tea, and Susie walked up the path to the front door with her heart thumping madly.

Mts Thomson welcomed Susie with a bright, warm smile and great concern. 'Take Susie upstairs to play,' suggested Mrs Thomson, 'while I get tea ready.'

Kiki's bedroom was a paradise. She had pine bunk beds with a whole range of matching furniture – a desk, wardrobe, toyboxes, everything. There was a separate computer desk with a monitor and keyboard all installed. The room looked as if it had fallen out of a magazine picture on The Best Way to Decorate.

'Do you like it?' asked Kiki. 'My uncle designed it. He did our kitchen too. He's designed rooms for pop-stars. You know Micky

Dunster of Blabbermouth? He's the singer. My uncle designed his whole house. Do you want a go on the computer?'

Susie sat down and played a few games while Kiki chattered away until there was a call from below and they went down for tea. Mrs Thomson had provided everything. It was more like a party than a tea and Susie enjoyed it despite herself. She began to relax.

'I was sorry to hear about your father leaving home,' said Mrs Thomson, flashing her big warm smile.

'I'm sorry too,' chipped in Kiki.

'I can understand why you told everyone he'd been run over.'

'So can I,' added Kiki. 'Mummy explained it to me and you were probably embarrassed.'

'Kiki . . .' murmured Mrs Thomson gently. 'But you mustn't feel embarrassed because we do understand and you can come and play here any time you like.' Mrs Thomson finished pouring out more lemonade and looked across at Susie who was sitting there quiter stunned.

What was this? Some kind of fairy-tale? She

managed to murmer a thank you. Why were all these people being helpful and understanding? They didn't understand at all and they were being sympathetic about the wrong things. It was all too confusing.

Susie was glad when she was able to walk home by herself. It was the first opportunity she'd had all day to be alone and she was grateful for it.

There was the river and there was there was the long, high hill. Susie found herself wondering if John was up there on the hill, climbing the rope. What strange people she knew – John and Kiki. One she hardly saw at all but shared about the only good thing in the village with – the rope. And the other, Susie could hardly get rid of and seemed to want to share all the bad things in Susie's life, like all her problems.

When she reached home Mrs Bonner handed her a letter. It was from Marsha.

Dear Susie,

Great news! Mum says I can come and stay during half term and it's only a week and a bit to go. I can't wait to see you again. I went swimming with Lisa yesterday. If it's hot we can go behind

the giant waterfall and catch giant lobsters. I'm getting fed up here and my brother is going to get murdered soon he broke all my new felt tip pens.
Lots of love, Marsha.
P.S. Lisa has got two Dutch Rabbits.

'That will be something to look forward to, won't it? Did you have a good time at Kiki's?'

'Her house is like a palace. Did you know her bedroom was designed by her uncle who designed a whole house for a pop-star?'

'Fancy that.'

'And she's got bunk beds and her own TV and computer and everything.'

Mrs Bonner laughed. 'And we've got Oscar! The greatest fish in all the world. Isn't it good to have a man in the house?'

Susie's heart lurched. Had Dad suddenly returned, while she'd been having tea at Kiki's?

'Who? What man?' squeaked Susie.

'Oscar, of course - brave, handsome, tall, hard-working Oscar!' cried Mrs Bonner, tapping the glass tank. 'One of these days I'm going to have him fried with chips.

Chapter Seven

Problems

The next week passed without much happening. Kiki slowly became tired of walking round like Susie's personal security guard and anyway, Mark and Alan didn't keep up their teasing for long. They were soon distracted by the good weather and better things to do. Susie was left to herself. On the whole she liked it that way, but sometimes she sat at the edge of the playground and watched the others racing round and laughing and she wanted to be part of it. But no one came over. Nobody asked her and she stayed alone.

One lunchtime she was sitting by herself doing nothing at all when a shadow fell across her lap and stopped. Susie looked up, squinting into the sunlight, and there was John.

'That was you, wasn't it?' he said, hands deep in his pockets and his thin head tilted slightly to one side.

'What was?'

'That stick on the rope. You put it there, didn't you?'

'What if I did?'

'Was you, wasn't it?' insisted John.

'So what?'

John wheeled away. 'Thought so,' he cast over his shoulder.

Susie watched him until he was on the far side of the playground. She had practically forgotten about the rope and the tree, what with everything else she'd had on her mind. She decided to go up there straight after school. Maybe John had ruined the rope – cut it down, or something.

When she reached the hilltop, Susie saw at once that the rope was still there and so was the stick. She swung back and launched herself into the wind. Her body twisted round and round while she waited for the rope to stop swinging completely. She hung there turning slowly, threw back her head and looked up at the branches.

There was a plank up there. Susie was certain it had not been there before. It was wedged across two thick branches to make a flat seat, right next to the rope. Susie stood on the stick and tried to climb the rope, but just as before she couldn't grab it with her feet which waved about beneath her, as useless as jellies.

She let go and fell to the ground, catching her chin on the stick-seat as it jerked upwards. Susie buried her chin in one hand and held it. There wasn't any blood, but it throbbed painfully and she knew she would have a big bruise there soon. It was enough to put her off the rope for the time being. There was no way Susie was going to be able to reach that plank. She clumped angrily home.

'Hallo – been in a boxing match?' asked Mrs Bonner, tilting Susie's chin for a better look. 'Who hit you?'

'It was a stick and it was an accident. I was by myself.'

'Put some of this on,' said her mother, handing over some cotton-wool and witch-hazel. 'That's supposed to be good for bruises.'

'It stinks,' complained Susie, wrinkling her nose.

Mrs Bonner ignored her. 'I've borrowed a camp bed from a neighbour and put it in your room for Marsha to sleep on. Okay?'

'You bet!' Susie raced upstairs and almost fell over the camp bed, because it took up nearly all the floor space in her little bedroom. Susie wished she had bunk beds like Kiki, but it didn't matter really. She lay down on the camp bed herself and was surprised how hard it felt. Then she sat up and wondered what it would be like when Marsha came.

There had been a time when they shared almost every moment of their lives. If Susie wasn't round at Marsha's house, then Marsha was round at Susie's, or they were out in the street together, racing round, playing jokes on people, building secret hideouts. They would plan what to do that afternoon, the next day, the next year, even what they'd do when they grew up. They were going to buy houses next to each other and have children at the same time so that they could play with each other just as Susie and Marsha had done.

Then suddenly Susie's dad went. There was no warning. Mrs Bonner came in from work one afternoon and found most of his things gone. Later that evening he rang up and told her that he'd moved out and gone to live with somebody else. Mum had screamed at him down the phone and called him every name under the sun, while Susie sat pretending to watch television. Mum had demanded to know what he was going to do about Susie. It was better this way, he'd said. Then Susie's mother had put the phone down and cried and Susie sat as still as still because she didn't know what to do.

After a while her mother had stopped crying and got up and said why should she be crying? She was better off without him. They were both better off without him.

Susie was not so sure, and could not help thinking that she was most of the problem herself. Maybe she'd even made Dad go off like that, although she couldn't think what she'd done.

Susie talked to Marsha about it. Marsha listened and nodded and didn't say much but Susie was sure Marsha understood, and she felt a lot better being able to talk about it freely.

Now Susie smiled to herself. Marsha was coming soon. It would be just like old times. She glanced through Marsha's letter and wondered how she would handle this business of the waterfall and the lobsters. Oh well, Marsha would understand! Then there was that bit about Lisa Edwards – no, two bits. Susie had always felt a bit jealous of Lisa. She went downstairs thoughtfully.

'What are Dutch rabbits, Mum?'

'I suppose they come from Holland. I don't know, love. Maybe they have ears like windmills or tulips. They come from Holland don't they? Perhaps they can speak Dutch.'

Susie paused. 'How long is Marsha coming for?'

'Two nights.'

'Two! Can't she stay longer than that?'

'Not this time. Her family are going up north to visit her aunt.'

'I'd rather go and stay at her place,' said Susie, secretly thinking that would get her out of the waterfall problem.

'Perhaps you can, next time. What do you miss most here, Marsha or the town?'

Susie frowned gloomily. 'Everything. I wish I didn't live in this crummy house or have to go to that crummy school. Why can't we go back? Why do we have to live here?'

Susie knew perfectly well why. After Dad had left, Mum decided she wanted to break with everything. She arranged a house swap through the council and three months after Dad had gone Susie and her mother had moved to the village.

Mrs Bonner looked at her daughter with a cheerful smile, 'You'll get used to it Susie. It's only because you haven't got any friends here yet.'

'I don't want any friends here.'

'I know it's quiet, but it is lovely here. It's great to be surrounded by countryside instead of all those horrible dirty buildings.'

'It's dead,' Susie muttered.

Mrs Bonner looked at her daughter. She felt much the same. 'Okay – making friends is difficult here. People haven't got used to us yet. What about Kiki? She's your friend, isn't she? I thought you went to tea with her.'

'She's all right, but not like Marsha. She's bossy.'

'Bossy?'

'No, not bossy, but I don't know how to describe it.'

'I was thinking of asking her here to tea,' suggested Mrs Bonner.

'No!'

'It was only an idea.'

Susie was horrified. The thought of Kiki coming into her grotty house and seeing her bedroom was awful. She's rather die. Mrs Bonner was laughing.

'I know what you're thinking. Kiki won't even notice. Let's have her round to tea.'

'No!' shouted Susie. 'I don't want her coming here!' Susie knew perfectly well that Kiki certainly would notice. She couldn't help but notice the difference between her designer bedroom and Susie's little room which didn't even have a carpet because Mrs Bonner didn't have enough money for one.

'Okay, suit yourself,' said her mother, 'but you mustn't expect all your friends to be like Marsha. You'll never make new friends if you do. People are all different.'

Susie went out. She didn't want to make friends. She had her own friend already, her very best friend Marsha. Marsha understood everything and nobody here in the village understood anything at all, not even Mum, who was too busy wrapped up in her own world to notice anything else. Well, when Marsha came it would be alright.

Chapter Eight

Crayfish and Boa-constrictor

It was odd seeing Marsha again. She came down by bus with her mother and when they got off Susie and Marsha just stood there and grinned. They went to a cafe nearby for coffee. Then Marsha's mother caught the bus back to town, while Susie and Marsha and Mrs Bonner climbed on to a different bus to take them out to the village.

'This is great,' said Marsha. 'It's a real adventure. What's your house like?'

'Okay,' said Susie, and she stared out of the window and pointed out bits that she recognoised. 'There was an accident on this corner last week. A car hit the bus because it's so big and the road is narrow. The bus is always getting hit.' It sounded exciting but the truth was it was quite boring when you had to sit and wait for half an hour while all the accident details were sorted out between the two drivers.

'Lisa Edwards' brother had an accident,' said Marsha, turning to her friend. 'He fell out of the window and knocked out his front teeth and broke his arm.'

'A boy at our school had an accident,' Susie invented hurriedly.

'What happened to him?'

'Oh, he um, he got hit by a car and broke both legs.' Susie cursed herself, her tongue and her imagination.

'Poor boy,' muttered Marsha. 'That's awful. Can he walk?'

'Only on crutches. He may never walk again.' Susie winced inside.

There was a long silence from Marsha.

'We wrote all over Tony's plaster,' she said. 'There was this plaster on his arm and we wrote things on it.'

'Did you?' murmered Susie, and she stared out of the window again at the pasing hedges and fields.

Marsha was quite impressed by the house,

even though Susie's room didn't have bunk beds, a TV or a carpet. Marsha didn't even notice and Susie was pleased. Her friend looked out of the window at the high hill.

'It's a lovely view,' she said. 'I wish I lived here.'

Susie smiled and kept quiet. She was beginning to wonder what she would do in the morning when Marsha wanted to see the waterfall. Susie wished she had never written those letters and she hated Marsha for having read them.

The two girls stayed up half the night, talking. Susie went on and on about her mum and dad. Marsha laughed when Susie said her mother kept talking to the fish and Susie wished that Marsha hadn't. It wasn't funny at all.

In the morning, as soon as breakfast was over, Marsha wanted to go down to the waterfall.

'Shall I put on my swimming gear? I brought it with me.'

'Have you got any wellies?' asked Susie in a

flat voice.

The two girls marched down to the river, with Susie marching very slowly.

'Is this the river?' asked Marsha.

'Yeah.'

'I thought it would be deeper and wider than this − you know − like a real river.'

'It is a real river,' said Susie crossly.

'Yeah, I know, but you know . . .'

They got to the floodgate where the mini-waterfall was. The water was rushing over the top of the gate and plunging a couple of feet into the river, where it foamed in little eddies. Marsha walked straight past and on, up the road.

'Come on!' she cried.

Susie leaned over the railings by the water's edge. 'It's here,' she said quietly, a funny feeling like being sick in her throat.

Marsha came running back and joined her friend by the river. 'Where? Where is it, I can't see any waterfall.'

'That's it!' shouted Susie, suddenly very cross, jerking her head towards the floodgate.

'Over there!'

Marsha looked at the cascading water. She looked above it and below it and either side of it and there was no way that she could make out a waterfall that you could stand behind.

'That's not it,' she cried.

'Yes it is.'

'No it isn't. You can't stand behind that piddling little thing.'

'So what?' cried Susie.

'You'd have to be a dwarf to stand behind that.'

'So what!'

'Is that really it?' Marsha could still hardly believe what she was seeing.

'Yeah, that's it.'

'You said there was a waterfall that you could stand behind.'

Susie was silent. She stared at the passing water and wished she could float away on the current, away from everything.

'Let's go somewhere else,' muttered Marsha eventually.

'Where?'

'Let's go to those rapids you wrote about, where the water's all wild and you can get smashed up on the rocks.'

Susie didn't move. Her heart now felt like a cold piece of plasticine. 'This is the rapids,' she said, and looking down at the rushing water of the river as it raced below. Marsha looked down too, for a long time.

'These are rapids?'

'Yes!' shouted Susie.

Marsha picked up a little twig and threw it into the water. It bobbed up and down, bouncing on the waves and rushing away to the stone bridge and beyond. 'Some rapids,' she said.

There was another long silence, until Susie climbed through the railings and waded into the water.

'Let's catch some crayfish,' she suggested.

'I don't suppose there are any,' said Marsha tartly, sticking to where she was. 'Anyway, I'm not bothered.'

Susie waded through the water, bending forward and turning over stone after stone, praying for a crayfish to appear. Marsha watched her coldly.

'There aren't any. You made it up, like every-thing else. You were lying. You're a liar. There aren't any crayfish.'

'There are! I just missed one,' cried Susie, as she lunged forward, almost falling in the water to snatch at a crayfish as it darted away to a new hiding place.

'Oh give up and stop pretending,' moaned Marsha.

'It's too difficult like this,' said Susie. 'The proper way is to use a jar and some bacon. The crayfish rush into the jar to get the bacon and then you whip the jar out of the water and you've got one. I caught over twenty like that the other day. It's dead easy.'

Marsha almost fell off the railings laughing. 'You don't expect me to believe that! Crayfish eating bacon in jam-jars! Oh wow Susie, you can really tell some big ones when you want to!'

Susie scrabbled amongst the stones on the bed of the river, but the crayfish were keeping well out of sight.

'I'm not lying! It's true!'

Marsha turned away in disgust and began to go back up the road. Susie ran after her, leaving a trail of wet footprints behind. 'Where are you going?' Susie asked.

Marsha shrugged and Susie walked alongside, wondering how to appease her friend. Marsha suddenly said. 'Lisa Edwards has got an uncle and he's got a boa-constrictor.'

'What's that?'

'A snake. It's as thick as my leg and it eats live mice.

'Urgh.'

'I've seen it. I saw it have lunch one day.'

'Urgh. How could you?'

There was another long silence. They were getting near Susie's house. She was desperate to make things right with Marsha and all at once she had a brainwave.

'Let's go up the hill. There's as rope up there that we can swing on. It's ace!'

'I know. You told me in your letter. And a tree-house.'

Susie shook her head. 'No there isn't. Not a

proper tree-house, only a plank, but it's really good.'

'You're only lying – like the waterfall and everything. I don't believe you any more. You're a liar.'

'But there is, honest. There's a rope and you can swing for ages because it's got a stick to sit on.'

Marsha grunted and turned up the path to the house. She went indoors. Susie sat down on the garden wall and looked at her feet. This was great, truly great. Fir the first time since she had moved, Susie's eyes filled with tears. They dropped silently on to the pavement and made wet stains beside her boots.

Chapter Nine

Friends

Susie sat on the garden wall. Her tears slowly dried, leaving smudged trails on her face. Maybe Marsha didn't want to go up the hill, but that need not stop her. She had not lied all the time — there *was* a tree and a rope and a plank, and Susie was going to go up there and swing and climb and Marsha could sit indoors and die of boredom for all Susie cared.

Susie jumped up and hurried to the footpath that led up the hill. Once again the houses slipped behind and grew smaller and smaller while the trees on top of the hill grew larger and larger. It was changing one world for another. There were only birds to break the quiet, and the sound of a slow wind trickling through the trees like dry water.

The rope was hanging almost still, faintly moved from time to time by tiny gusts of air.

Susie ran over and a moment later she was swinging through the air with her feet thrust out in front and her hair streaming behind.

'I'm flying!' she announced to the silent forest. 'I'm a bird!'

Then she had another go at climbing the rope.

She could not get the hang of it. She tried again and again, but it was useless. She stood by the rope and idly swung it by hand, caught it, and swung it again.

'I can fly! I'm a bird!' shouted a voice, and there was John. He was standing on the plank. He must have been lying up there all the time, out of sight, all the while Susie was swinging and trying to climb. Now he was standing there grinning like a toothpaste advert and flapping his arms.

'I can fly! Tweet! Tweet! I'm a bird!' he cried, and he looked down at her. 'You're a wally!'

Susie eyed him angrily. 'I didn't know you were up there.'

'I know you didn't. Hidden, wasn't I?' He grinned at her, grabbed the rope and slid to the ground. Susie began to back away, but he didn't come after her.

It's no wonder you can't climb this thing. You haven't got your feet right. You've got to grip with 'em see?' John placed his feet carefully round the rope, so that one foot trapped the rope against the other. He jumped down and swung the rope across to Susie. 'Go on. You do it. Take the stick off first and it'll be easier because the rope will be longer.'

Susie untied the stick so that the rope almost touched the ground. She grabbed it and flapped round madly with her feet.

'Come here,' said John impatiently, grabbing the rope from her.

'Look, you jump up and I'll put your feet in the right place.'

Susie did as she was told without saying a word. She held tight while John grabbed her flying feet.

'Ow! Can't you stop kicking me? Put that one there – no! Keep it there you wally! Now the rope goes there and – aarrgh!' He gave a startled yell as Susie let go and collapsed in a heap on top of him. They rolled to the ground.

'You plonker!' shouted John.

'Birdbrain! I couldn't hold on any longer,' Susie cried. They stared at each other and brushed dirt and leaves from their clothes.

'Have another go,' growled John. He was determined Susie should succeed. If she failed now it would be his failure too. 'And try and hold on longer this time will you? You weigh a ton!'

'Thanks a million,' muttered Susie. grabbing the rope once more.

This time she was more successful and John was shouting. 'That's it! Now move your hands up. Now slide your feet up. Go on, go on . . .'

'I can't! I'm too high – I'll fall!'

'No you won't, wally. Just jump down.'

Susie jumped and landed at his feet. She stood there panting and grinning. 'How high did I get?'

'Have another go,' said John.

Susie managed to get almost to the top of the rope, but her arms were not used to all that pulling and she got scared as she saw the ground getting further and further away. She wondered how she would ever get back down without actually falling and breaking her neck. At last John said he was going home for lunch and without another word he sloped off down the hill. Susie had a couple more goes, just to prove that she could climb without his help, and then she went back home too.

Mrs Bonner was angry because Marsha had been left in the house with nobody to play with. Susie didn't see what the fuss was about. It was Marsha who had walked off first, not her. The two girls sat through lunch with hardly a word between them.

'What's wrong with you two then?' asked Mrs Bonner.

'Nothing,' mumbled Susie.

'I'm bored,' Marsha said, picking at her lunch.

Mrs Bonner looked at her daughter and Susie rolled her eyes in despair.

After lunch Mrs Bonner told Susie she would have to stay with Marsha. 'She is your best friend after all,' she pointed out. Susie had another go at getting Marsha to come up the hill.

'It's really good up there.' she kept saying, but Marsha would have none of it.

'You're a liar. There's nothing up there. You lied about the river and the waterfall and everything and I don't believe you any more.'

There wasn't much conversation after that. The two girls wandered about the village but hardly said a word to each other. It was obvious to both of them that something big had changed in their lives. Marsha was homesick and Susie was bitter. Somehow they got through the evening and when Marsha woke next morning it was time to pack and catch the bus back to meet her mother and go home.

The girls waved to each other at the bus station as Marsha's bus left. Susie knew that it was probably the last time she would see Marsha. She felt sad and relieved at the same time. She sat in silence at the back of the village bus with her mother and it was not until they reached home that Mrs Bonner said anything.

She got the tub of fish food and sprinkled some on to the water. 'Well Oscar, I thought I didn't understand men, but I don't understand girls either. I thought her best friend would cheer her up. Instead she's moping around like an old dishcloth. Oscar? Are you listening to me?' Mrs Bonner knocked the side of the tank, while Oscar ignored her and concentrated on the slow task of hoovering up all the floating flakes of fish food.

'He's a brilliant talker,' muttered Mrs Bonner, looking across at her daughter. 'So, what are you going to do now?'

'Going down to the river to catch crayfish,' said Susie.

'I didn't mean that. You've bored Marsha stiff. I don't suppose she'll come back here.'

'That's okay. I don't want to go to her place anyhow.'

'I thought you were best friends?'

Susie looked at the floor, unable to bring herself to say they weren't friends any longer.

Mrs Bonner nodded. 'All right, catch your bloomin' crayfish. Why don't you bring one back and we'll put it in with Oscar. Maybe it will liven him up.'

Susie took the jam jar and the string and a

small piece of bacon. Soon she was wading about the river getting soaked. She forgot about Marsha in the excitement of chasing crayfish. She caught at least seven before she found one that she felt was big enough to take home and then she marched up the road in triumph.

Mrs Bonner was surprised and delighted. She gently lowered the creature into Oscar's tank, where the crayfish immediately sank to the bottom and hid beneath a large stone.

Oscar drifted lower, his big mouth glooping at the stone. There was a flurry of dirt from the bottom as the crayfish shot out, grabbed Oscar's lower lip in one pincer and just as quickly flashed back under the stone. Oscar shot off in the opposite direction, opening and shutting his mouth, in a state of shock. Mrs Bonner fell about laughing.

'Oh Susie! Look at him, just look at him! What a shock! That crayfish must be a female, the way she got him. Well done, little crayfish! I think we'll call you Mavis.'

'Mavis?' echoed Susie in despair.

'Yeah, look at him. He's still scared. Mavis —

you're a pal!'

Susie crouched down and watched the tank, while Oscar slowly circled round, keeping well clear of the terrifying stone at the bottom. 'Shall I get another crayfish?' asked Susie.

Mrs Bonner shook her head. 'No. Mavis is quite enough for poor old Oscar. She'll keep him on his toes.'

'On his fins,' said Susie

'Yeah.'

'You're mad Mum.'

'Yeah, I know.'

As Susie closed the curtains that night she saw the hill from her window, with the trees on the top dark against a dark sky. It was good to have the room to herself once more. The camp bed was gone. Marsha's things had gone and so had Marsha. Anyway, Susie thought, I'm not a liar. There is a waterfall, and crayfish, and a tree, and a blank and a rope, and it's amazing.

And there was John, and maybe even Kiki – but not until Susie could climb right to the top of that rope and sit on the plank, Queen of the Forest.

ABOUT THE AUTHOR

Jeremy Strong lives near Bath on the site of an extinct volcano. After many years as a teacher and a headmaster, he has become one of our most popular and amusing writers.

Many of Jeremy's books have been short listed for prizes and several have won, most recently, The Hundred Mile an Hour Dog, which was given the Children's Book Award.

Jeremy Strong's main hobbies are sleeping and eating as many different kinds of bread as he can find.